REBUILDING TRUST

TRAUMA SERIES

21 DAY DEVOTIONAL

BY TAMI RENE'

I Dedicate this devotional to all the brokenhearted seeking healing. TRD

Table of Contents

Forward

This is TRULY a powerful devotional! It's so filled with the Truth of Gods Word and open enough to leave room for the healing power of the Holy Spirit to give you a refreshed hope in God's good will for your life!

As a Christian woman who has endured life's heartbreaks and been lovingly rescued countless times by the hand of God, I truly appreciate God leading Tami to pen such a dynamic correlation of suffering and trust. It's not always easy to see how disappointments, setbacks, offenses, and trauma can easily, and often insidiously, cause our outlook and expectations of God to become skewed and off-center.

It took me a long time to not project onto my Heavenly Father the negative and toxic experiences that I had with my earthly father. As a result, I felt accomplished to know OF God, yet I dared not venture with Him beyond the surface, because I had not yet come to know how God would be any different than the human father who was supposed to love and care for me just the same.

Here's the truth:
When our hearts are broken and we feel let down, it's very easy to become unaware of the fullness and Truth of God's perfect love for us. Walking through the darkest nights and the hottest fires of life can leave us with a default attitude of cynicism, skepticism,

and more than likely, a battered and worn out sense of faith. And if we're really bold, like some of our predecessors in the Bible, we'll even go as far as to ask questions like, "God, why did you let this happen?"... "Why me?"... "Where were you?"... and so on.

Yet, Jesus' profound and deep love for us has a way of locating and even comprehending the real meaning in our questions, doubts, and fears. He hears our worries. He feels our confusion. And He answers us through the inspired words recorded in the Bible.

That's why this devotional is so powerful! Tami has done an impeccable job at highlighting the deepness of the Word of God that relates to the various stages of trust recovery and inner healing. The Scriptures, prayers, and moments of reflections are all a very necessary part of the healing and restoration journey.

This is YOUR time for healing and deliverance. Approach this sacred journey with the Lord with joy and great expectation.

Abide, soak, and settle in the Truth that "The Lord is close to the brokenhearted and saves those who are crushed in spirit." (Psalm 34:18)

Healing and revival is yours in Christ.

"Trust in the LORD with all your heart..." (Proverbs 3:5-6)

Dee Bryant

Christian Women Mindset & Business Mentor

www.womanyouareloved.com

Introduction

This 21 day devotional is meant to take you deeper into the Heart of God to re-establish trust where variations of life's traumas and trials have brought doubt. I have not added commentaries except personalized prayers so the focus is on His Scriptures and Him speaking to you personally through them.

For the Lord Jesus Christ came and died for us all to be healed in our spirits, souls and bodies. One of the biggest areas that is effected by trauma is in the area of trust. For it effects our mind and emotions. Trauma erodes our trust and perspectives of our Father in Heaven, others and ourselves.

He is truly the only Trustworthy One and our relationship with Him is what brings us understanding of our true identity and healing transformation.

This devotional is designed to get you to that place of hearing His Voice in the Scriptures and in that still small whisper and of how much He loves you and how touched He is by your pain and infirmities. He so desperately wants you to be restored to Him fully and walk in wholeness. This is to help on your journey to go deeper with God and restoration in your true identity.

Why journal and Dialogue with God?
1. To be saturated in prayer through the Bible and quiet time listening to His response to you (Psalm 119:15)

2. Offer your faith filled petitions by being specific in your needs (Psalm 20:5)

3. Tell Him every detail of your life & sit quietly to receive His tender words of mercy, love, kindness, insight and wisdom for your life. (Hebrews 4:16)

4. Learn to get deeper revelation and understanding from the Scriptures of who He really is as He speaks to you through them and you learn to apply the Word to your life. (James 1:22)

"Don't be pulled in different directions or worried about a thing. Be saturated in prayer throughout each day, offering your faith-filled requests before God with overflowing gratitude. Tell him every detail of your life, then God's wonderful peace that transcends human understanding, will make the answers known to you through Jesus Christ. So keep your thoughts continually fixed on all that is authentic and real, honorable and admirable, beautiful and respectful, pure and holy, merciful and kind. And fasten your thoughts on every glorious work of God, praising him always. Philippians 4:6-8 TPT

Day 1:
Safe and Secure

"When you sit enthroned under the shadow of Shaddai, you are hidden in the strength of God Most High. He's the hope that holds me and the Stronghold to shelter me, the only God for me, and my great confidence."
Psalms 91:1-2 TPT

Personalized Prayer:

When I sit enthroned under Your shadow Father, I am hidden in the Almighty One, my strength. You are the hope that holds me and my only Stronghold that shelters me. You are the only God for me! You are the only Trustworthy One and and in You is my greatest confidence!

Conversation:

1. Start the dialogue with Father God by writing out your own Personalized Prayer or use the one provided. (Include thankfulness for who He is)

2. As you sit quietly with the Lord ask Him if there is any beliefs about Him that may be hindering you from entering His shelter for you.

3. Ask the Lord how these verses apply to you directly today.

4. Ask the Lord is there any action you should take in response to the verses. (Can be abstract like hope)

Day 2:
Safe and Secure

"He will rescue you from every hidden trap of the enemy, and He will protect you from false accusation and any deadly curse. His massive arms are wrapped around you, protecting you. You can run under His covering of majesty and hide. His arms of faithfulness are a shield keeping you from harm."
Psalms 91:3-4 TPT

Personalized Prayer:

Thank you Father that You rescue me from every trap of the enemy of my soul and You protect me from every time he attacks to erode my trust in You, myself and others. Your massive arms wrap around me, protecting me. Every time I run under Your covering of safety and security You are faithful to shield me from harm. Empower me to see from Your perspective.

Conversation:

1. Start the dialogue with Father God by writing out your own Personalized Prayer or use the one provided. (Include thankfulness for who He is)

2. Is there any other additions to this prayer that you feel the Lord speaking to you about His love and protection?

3. Ask the Lord how these verses apply to you directly today.

4. Ask the Lord is there any action you should take in response to the verses. (Can be abstract like hope)

Day 3:
Safe and Secure

"God sends angels with special orders to protect you wherever you go, defending you from all harm. If you walk into a trap, they'll be there for you and keep you from stumbling."
Psalms 91:11-12 TPT

Personalized Prayer:

Thank you Father! I am so grateful and amazed that You send angels with special orders to protect me wherever I go, defending me from all harm. Even if I walk into a trap, or do not understand, You are always directing my paths to keep me from stumbling! I surrender to Your love and kindness and untold mercies for me today! Thank You for insight today that when I learn to cry out to You, You are faithful to respond!

Conversation:

1. Start the dialogue with Father God by writing out your own Personalized Prayer or use the one provided. (Include thankfulness for who He is)

2. Ask the Lord any situations that you can surrender to Him when you have not felt protected and lay them at His feet and break any agreement with the lie that He does not desire to protect you.

3. Ask the Lord how these verses apply to you directly concerning His promises to protect your heart in all circumstances.

4. Ask the Lord is there any action you should take in response to the verses. (Can be abstract like hope)

Day 4:
Song of Trust

"In your day of danger may the Lord answer and deliver you. May the name of the God of Jacob set you safely on high! May supernatural help be sent from His sanctuary. May He support you from Zion's fortress! May He remember every gift you have given Him and celebrate every sacrifice of love you have shown Him. Pause in His presence". Psalm 20:1-3 TPT

Personalized Prayer:

Thank You Father that in my times of danger I cry out to You and You answer and deliver me. You keep me safely in the Secret place with You. You are quick to send help on my behalf and always protect my heart inside Yours no matter what happens. Every time I choose to love You even when it is hard, is a sweet fragrance to You and You celebrate my love for You. I choose to trust in You to protect my heart and mind.

Conversation:

1. Start the dialogue with Father God by writing out your own Personalized Prayer or use the one provided. (Include thankfulness for who He is)

2. Ask the Lord for a "picture" of the Secret place He has set aside just for you and describe it and how you "feel".

3. Ask the Lord how these verses apply to the place He is showing you and how often can you access that?

4. Ask the Lord is there any action you should take in response to the verses. (Can be abstract like hope)

Day 5:
A Song of Trust

"May God give you every desire of your heart and carry out your every plan as you go to battle. When you succeed, we will celebrate and shout for joy! Flags will fly when victory is yours! Yes, God will answer your prayers and we will praise h Him! I know God gives me all that I ask for and brings victory to His anointed king. My deliverance cry will be heard in His holy heaven. By His mighty hand miracles will manifest through His saving strength."
Psalms 20:4-6 TPT

Personalized Prayer:

Thank you Father that You alone give me the desires of my heart. Because You have placed them there, You also give me victory every time I go to battle to establish my desire for full trust in You in my life. When I succeed You are the first one to shout for joy over me! I know that Your heart is always for me and brings me victory, for You are my Anointed King. You hear all my cries for deliverance in Your Holy Heaven and You stretch out Your mighty hand of strength to save me from the schemes of the enemy!

Conversation:

1. Start the dialogue with Father God by writing out your own Personalized Prayer or use the one provided. (Include thankfulness for who He is)

2. As you quietly sit with the Lord ask Him the words of joy and victory that He shouts over you!

3. Ask the Lord how these verses apply to you directly today.

4. Ask the Lord is there any action you should take in response to the verses. (Can be abstract like hope)

Day 6:
A Song of Trust

"Some find their strength in their weapons and wisdom, but my miracle deliverance can never be won by men. Our boast is in the Lord our God, who makes us strong and gives us victory! Our enemies will not prevail; they will only collapse and perish in defeat while we will rise up, full of courage. Give victory to our King, O God! The day we call on You, give us Your answer!"
Psalms 20:4, 7-9 TPT

Personalized Prayer:

Father, I thank You for reminding me to never put my trust in man nor get my identity from anyone but You! You are the only One that can deliver me and heal my wounds and satisfy that place in my heart only meant for You to fill. You always empower me by Your Spirit to push towards victory in every area of my life. When I call on You Lord, You always answer me! Thank you for Your faithfulness and tender mercies towards me. Thank You that I can come to You with the most inner most parts of me. Be vulnerable and You will never reject nor condemn me as I lay them at Your feet. You are so trustworthy.

Conversation:

1. Start the dialogue with Father God by writing out your own Personalized Prayer or use the one provided. (Include thankfulness for who He is)

2. Ask the Lord the times that you have put what people say over you that fell short of who God says you are. Forgive those people and than surrender those opinions of man to the Lord and than ask Him who He says you are. (Hint: it should be so wonderful it is even uncomfortable)

3. Write out with gratitude how you are wonderfully made.

4. Ask the Lord is there any action you should take in response to the verses. (Can be abstract like hope)

Day 7:
Growing in Intimacy

"I pray that the Father of glory, the God of our Lord Jesus Christ, would impart to you the riches of the Spirit of wisdom and the Spirit of revelation to know Him through your deepening intimacy with Him."
Ephesians 1:17 TPT

Personalized Prayer:

Thank you Father for Your Holy Spirit! Show me Lord how to come into agreement with You through Your wisdom and revelation so I can draw closer to You. Help me to trust You and learn what true heart to heart intimacy is. I break agreement with what the world has taught me about intimacy and desire for You to teach me! My heart yearns for this pure Holy Affection from Heaven to fill me to over flowing!

Conversation:

1. Start the dialogue with Father God by writing out your own Personalized Prayer or use the one provided. (Include thankfulness for who He is)

2. Ask the Lord the false beliefs you may have concerning true intimacy and the Holy affection that He desires you to experience.

3. Break agreement with any false beliefs from the world, your generational line and any other man made structure that does not line up with the truth of God's Spirit, Ways and Nature and ask Him to establish His Kingdom structures instead.

4. Ask the Lord is there any action you should take in response to the verse. (Can be abstract like hope)

Day 8:
Growing in Intimacy

"But continue to grow and increase in God's grace and intimacy with our Lord and Savior, Jesus Christ. May He receive all the glory both now and until the day eternity begins. Amen!"
2 Peter 3:18 TPT

Personalized Prayer:

Thank you Lord for this journey of growing from Glory to Glory in intimacy with You! Thank you Lord that it is not a one time event but an ever growing, ever expanding adventure into Your goodness, kindness and tender mercies. Help me Lord to be Your friend. To learn Your ways and nature. That when I read Your Scriptures they come alive and reveal You to me in an ever increasing depth.

Conversation:

1. Start the dialogue with Father God by writing out your own Personalized Prayer or use the one provided. (Include thankfulness for who He is)

2. Ask the Lord any areas of beliefs you may have that you have to perform or earn His love and surrender them to Him.

3. Acknowledge that from this day forward you are growing from Glory to Glory. That this is a wonderful journey of relationship with Him not just a one time event when you accepted Jesus as your Savior.

4. Ask the Lord is there any action you should take in response to the verses. (Can be abstract like hope)

Day 9:
Growing in Intimacy

"God, Your wrap-around Presence is our defense. In Your kindness look upon the faces of Your anointed ones. For just one day of intimacy with You is like a thousand days of joy rolled into one! I'd rather stand at the threshold in front of the Gate Beautiful, ready to go in and worship my God, than to live my life without You in the most beautiful palace of the wicked."

Psalms 84:9-10 TPT

Personalized Prayer:

Thank you Lord for Your Presence that wraps me in protection! Your goodness is a security and safety net for me! The joy I feel on the inside is more than I can contain at times! I weep feeling your protection and love for me. How could I have ever doubted You? You are always standing at the Gate Beautiful. The place of restoration, healing for my spirit, soul and body. I come to You today, kneel before You and receive all that You have for me to receive. Thank you that it is in these times that my mis-trust washes away in the Presence of the Trustworthy One!

Conversation:

1. Start the dialogue with Father God by writing out your own Personalized Prayer or use the one provided. (Include thankfulness for who He is)

2. Ask the Lord for you to feel and experience His Presence in a way you have not before.

3. Write down and express your gratefulness for what you are experiencing. It may be a feeling, He may touch your emotions, or show you a picture in your mind.

4. Ask the Lord is there any action you should take in response to the verses. (Can be abstract like hope)

Day 10:
Growing in Intimacy

"Farther than from a sunrise to a sunset— that's how far You've removed our guilt from us. The same way a loving father feels toward his children— that's but a sample of Your tender feelings toward us, Your beloved children, who live in awe of you. You know all about us, inside and out. You are mindful that we're made from dust."
Psalms 103:12-14 TPT

Personalized Prayer:

Father, not a moment of my life have You not seen. You have removed my guilt and shame and do not hold it against me. You have seen every time I was injured and my trust was shattered. I am Your beloved child who can run to You to heal and bind my heart up again. I am in awe of Your unfailing love for me. That I was created to be in relationship with You from the moment I was conceived in my mothers womb. I have always been Your idea and when You created me You said that it was very good!

Conversation:

1. Start the dialogue with Father God by writing out your own Personalized Prayer or use the one provided. (Include thankfulness for who He is)

2. Ask the Lord any areas of beliefs you may have that you have to perform or earn His love and surrender them to Him. Ask Him to heal these broken places that hinder your relationship with Him.

3. Write out truth of who you are as His beloved child.

4. Ask the Lord is there any action you should take in response to the verses. (Can be abstract like hope)

Day 11:
Growing in Intimacy

"Love is large and incredibly patient. Love is gentle and consistently kind to all. It refuses to be jealous when blessing comes to someone else. Love does not brag about one's achievements nor inflate its own importance. Love does not traffic in shame and disrespect, nor selfishly seek its own honor. Love is not easily irritated or quick to take offense. Love is a safe place of shelter, for it never stops believing the best for others. Love never takes failure as defeat, for it never gives up." 1 Corinthians 13:4-5, 7 TPT

Personalized Prayer:

Thank you Lord that You are teaching me what love and intimacy really is. That as I experience Your overwhelming love for me in Your patience, kindness and gentleness it displaces every place inside me where love was misrepresented to me in the world. Thank you that You are rebuilding a hedge of trust around me so I can learn to love from this deep well inside me where Your Spirit is abiding in me. Thank You Lord that my failures are never meant to defeat me, ever. That when others have failed me it was never meant to defeat me, ever. You always believe the best in me. I can trust You to never use them against me but to teach me to learn from them and You are always with me to help me let them go.

Conversation:

1. Start the dialogue with Father God by writing out your own Personalized Prayer or use the one provided. (Include thankfulness for who He is)

2. Ask the Lord to heal every time your borders of protection were assaulted. Release forgiveness to those that He shows you may have unintentionally or intentionally violated them

3. Ask the Lord to shore up every boundary and hedge of protection that was established for you in your mothers womb to be restored so a secure hedge of trust in God be secured from this day forward so

you can learn to truly love as you were intended to.

4. Ask the Lord is there any action you should take in response to the verses

Day 12:
His Love

"So now I live with the confidence that there is nothing in the universe with the power to separate us from God's love. I'm convinced that His love will triumph over death, life's troubles, fallen angels, or dark rulers in the heavens. There is nothing in our present or future circumstances that can weaken his love."
Romans 8:38 TPT

Personalized Prayer:

Thank you Father that I can continuously rely on You to help me overcome any obstacles I might face. I am becoming more convinced every moment of the day that Your love, Your sacrifice for me on the Cross is sufficient! That Your love for me, Your empowerment to me by Your Spirit, establishes complete trust in our relationship. Thank you for Your transformational power that enables me to be transformed into the image of Your dear Son Jesus, My Savior. That no weapon formed against me will prosper.

Conversation:

1. Start the dialogue with Father God by writing out your own Personalized Prayer or use the one provided. (Include thankfulness for who He is)

2. Ask the Lord any areas of mis trust you may have and surrender them to Him.

3. Ask Father for a fresh filling of His mighty Holy Spirit to empower you minute by minute and day by day to establish this unshakeable trust He desires for you.

4. Ask the Lord is there any action you should take in response to the verses. (Can be abstract like hope)

Day 13:
His Love

""I love each of you with the same love that the Father loves me. You must continually let My love nourish your hearts. If you keep My commands, you will live in My love, just as I have kept My Father's commands, for I continually live nourished and empowered by His love. My purpose for telling you these things is so that the joy that I experience will fill your hearts with overflowing gladness!"
John 15:9-11 TPT

Personalized Prayer:

Lord Jesus, I am so grateful for ALL that You have done for me! That You emptied Yourself to come and be born into a human body to not only pay the ultimate forever sacrifice for my complete salvation but be the "pattern Son" for me to follow to establish me into fellowship with Father as His child, so that I too can have such an overflowing gladness in my heart! Thank you that You are continually nourishing my heart as I seek You. I yield every place in my life that has broken trust to You today to heal, nourish and establish Your goodness and gladness in!

Conversation:

1. Start the dialogue with Father God by writing out your own Personalized Prayer or use the one provided. (Include thankfulness for who He is)

2. Ask the Lord any areas of beliefs you may have that you have to perform or earn His love and surrender them to Him.

3. Break any agreement with self rejection and ask the Lord for a simple Word strategy to declare throughout the day for His to be poured out in you to love Him and love others as yourself.

4. Ask the Lord is there any action you should take in response to the verses. (Can be abstract like hope)

Day 14:
His Love

"For here is eternal truth: When that time comes you won't need to ask Me for anything, but instead you will go directly to the Father and ask Him for anything you desire and He will give it to you, because of your relationship with Me. Until now you've not been bold enough to ask the Father for a single thing in My name, but now you can ask, and keep on asking Him! And you can be sure that you'll receive what you ask for, and your joy will have no limits!"
John 16:23-24 TPT

Personalized Prayer:

Thank you Jesus! Oh Father, I ask that every area of my heart that has been damaged through any event that violated my trust would You heal it now in Jesus Name! I come boldly to Your Throne of Grace through the precious Blood of Jesus and ask not only for healing Father, but recompense for every tear, every injured relationship and please rebuild my hedges of protection that is built on the Rock of Trust, Jesus Himself. I thank You Lord for all that You are doing to restore me to the fullness of the intended relationship You desire for us to have with each other in Jesus Name!

Conversation:

1. Start the dialogue with Father God by writing out your own Personalized Prayer or use the one provided. (Include thankfulness for who He is)

2. Ask the Lord any areas of beliefs you may have that you have to perform or earn His love and surrender them to Him. Acknowledge that through your relationship with Jesus you can come boldly to the Throne of Grace.

3. Ask Father for recompense for all that has been stolen from you. Be specific in your written request to Father.

4. Ask the Lord is there any action you should take in response to the verses. (Can be abstract like hope)

Day 15:
Identity

""My old identity has been co-crucified with Messiah and no longer lives; for the nails of His cross crucified me with Him. And now the essence of this new life is no longer mine, for the Anointed One lives His life through me— we live in union as one! My new life is empowered by the faith of the Son of God who loves me so much that He gave himself for me, and dispenses His life into mine!"
Galatians 2:20 TPT

Personalized Prayer:

Thank you Lord that I am a new creation! Old things have passed away! Because of Your sacrifice, Your precious Holy Spirit now lives in me as He did You while on earth. How marvelous is that! I do not have to live life on my own, as a slave to the things that kept me burdened. I am now Born of the Spirit. Brand new. Your love that is complete now flows to me and through me. I have been translated into Your Kingdom of Light through Your Dear Son Jesus!

Conversation:

1. Start the dialogue with Father God by writing out your own Personalized Prayer or use the one provided. (Include thankfulness for who He is)

2. Ask the Lord what does He mean by you being a New Creation?

3. Make a commitment to yourself today to take every thought captive that does not line up with who God says you and those close to you are. (Example: I reject that thought in Jesus Name)

4. Ask the Lord is there any action you should take in response to the verses. (Can be abstract like hope)

Day 16:
Identity

"Then God said, "Let Us make man in Our image, according to Our likeness; let them have dominion over the fish of the sea, over the birds of the air, and over the cattle, over all the earth and over every creeping thing that creeps on the earth." So God created man in His own image; in the image of God He created him; male and female He created them." Genesis 1:26-27 NKJV

Personalized Prayer:

Thank you Father that You created me in Your own image! That what you create is very good, unique, and that I was designed to be loved by You and in an unbreakable fellowship with You. Empower me by Your Spirit to comprehend this great and marvelous truth that is even deeper than what you established in the Garden because now I am in union with You.

Conversation:

1. Start the dialogue with Father God by writing out your own Personalized Prayer or use the one provided. (Include thankfulness for who He is)

2. Ask the Lord to reveal to you His Nature as He did Moses when He put him in the cleft of the rock.

3. Based on His Nature in Galatians 5:22-23 ask the Lord to show you even through all the trials of life how His nature towards you was in action.

4. Ask the Lord is there any action you should take in response to the verses. (Can be abstract like hope)

Day 17:
Identity

"For You formed my inward parts; You covered me in my mother's womb. I will praise You, for I am fearfully and wonderfully made; Marvelous are Your works, And that my soul knows very well. My frame was not hidden from You, When I was made in secret, And skillfully wrought in the lowest parts of the earth."
Psalms 139:13-15 NKJV

Personalized Prayer:

Thank you Father that from the moment of my conception You declared over me that I am wonderfully and fearfully made and that You see me as one of Your marvelous works. You designed me with the skill of the ultimate Creator. You God are my Father! My heart runs over with overwhelming love and awe at the thought of it. So grateful to You!

Conversation:

1. Start the dialogue with Father God by writing out your own Personalized Prayer or use the one provided. (Include thankfulness for who He is)

2. As you sit quietly ask Holy Spirit to search Father's heart and reveal to you how wonderful and marvelous that He made you.

3. Pour out your love, gratefulness and agreement with Father about who you really are.

4. Ask the Lord is there any action you should take in response to the verses. (Can be abstract like hope)

Day 18:
Identity

"Your eyes saw my substance, being yet unformed. And in Your book they all were written, The days fashioned for me, When as yet there were none of them. How precious also are Your thoughts to me, O God! How great is the sum of them! If I should count them, they would be more in number than the sand; When I awake, I am still with You."
Psalms 139:16-18 NKJV

Personalized Prayer:

Thank you Father that even as an unformed embryo in my mothers womb all the days of my life were written in a special book! That You have never taken Your eyes off of me for one second. That no matter life's trials You knew I would always choose You, You knew I would always run to You! Your thoughts towards me are always as a Father who has tender love for his child. There is nothing than can ever separate me from that love. When I sleep You minister to my heart. I pray to You before I drift off into slumber and You answer those prayers for healing in my soul.

Conversation:

1. Start the dialogue with Father God by writing out your own Personalized Prayer or use the one provided. (Include thankfulness for who He is)

2. Ask the Lord to reveal to you the blessing that you are designed to be to Him and to others.

3. Come into agreement through spoken and written words of your wonderful design and blessing you are to your Father. That you are created so uniquely and highly treasured.

4. Ask the Lord is there any action you should take in response to the verses. (Can be abstract like hope)

Day 19:
Rooted in Trust

"And then, after your brief suffering, the God of all loving grace, who has called you to share in His eternal glory in Christ, will personally and powerfully restore you and make you stronger than ever. Yes, He will set you firmly in place and build you up."
1 Peter 5:10 TPT

Personalized Prayer:

Thank you Lord that I have eternal glory in Christ Jesus! That You personally and powerfully are restoring me to the fullness in which You had intended when I was born into this world. That the foundation of Trust we have between us is secured in Jesus. That as I seek You, You are the one that establishes me upon the Rock of my Salvation. I can totally trust You to do this because You alone are the Author and finisher of my faith and no other!

Conversation:

1. Start the dialogue with Father God by writing out your own Personalized Prayer or use the one provided. (Include thankfulness for who He is)

2. Ask the Lord any areas of beliefs you may still be struggling with that hinder trust between you and surrender them to Him.

3. Declare through your spoken and written words a declaration of trust that Jesus established with you at the Cross and no person, place or thing can ever change that.

4. Ask the Lord is there any action you should take in response to the verses. (Can be abstract like hope)

Day 20:
Rooted in Trust

"For we have already experienced "heart-circumcision," and we worship God in the power and freedom of the Holy Spirit, not in laws and religious duties. We are those who boast in what Jesus Christ has done, and not in what we can accomplish in our own strength."
Philippians 3:3 TPT

Personalized Prayer:

Thank you Lord that You desire and perform the circumcision of my heart so it is tender to You! Thank you that I am now empowered by Your Spirit of Holiness that enables me to be transformed and taken from Glory to Glory! Thank you for the testimony of Jesus in my life that has built such a fortress of trust with You that my life is a witness to Your faithfulness and goodness and glory!

Conversation:

1. Start the dialogue with Father God by writing out your own Personalized Prayer or use the one provided. (Include thankfulness for who He is)

2. Ask the Lord if there are any areas of your heart that yet need to be tenderized by Him.

3. Thank Him in deep gratitude that He is trustworthy with your heart. Pour out your heart to Him for being your Fortress of Trust.

4. Ask the Lord is there any action you should take in response to the verses. (Can be abstract like hope)

Day 21:
Rooted in Trust

"Then you will be empowered to discover what every holy one experiences—the great magnitude of the astonishing love of Christ in all its dimensions. How deeply intimate and far-reaching is His love! How enduring and inclusive it is! Endless love beyond measurement that transcends our understanding—this extravagant love pours into you until you are filled to overflowing with the fullness of God!"
Ephesians 3:18-19 TPT

Personalized Prayer:

Thank you Father that I am accepted in the Beloved as a holy one. That the great magnitude of Your love as washed away every trace of mistrust in my life. That You pluck out what harms me and plant Your everlasting over flowing love into every hole! Your love so overwhelms me that my natural mind can not contain it! Increase my faith Papa to hold more, to believe more, to embrace more of Your redemptive love. I desire to carry Your fullness in my life so Jesus gets His full reward for what He paid for. I desire to express Your heart to others as the unique person You designed me to be. I love and trust You with all my heart. You are worthy of my trust oh God.

Conversation:

1. Start the dialogue with Father God by writing out your own Personalized Prayer or use the one provided. (Include thankfulness for who He is)

2. As you listen quietly today, ask Him to pour His Holy Love into you so deeply that you are forever changed. Spend time with your Father in Heaven as He whispers his love, acceptance, and identity into you.

My Prayer for you:

Father thank you that Your Beloved One is forever changed by the last 21 days of pressing into your love for them. That they continue in this wonderful intimate relational journey with You that over shadows all else. Thank you Lord that Jesus is enthroned deeper into the heart of this precious Holy One. That You are truly the only Author and Finisher of their faith and that not one of Your children can be snatched from Your Hand. Amen.

Art By Allison Teal Lewis: Tealpatrickart.com

Additional resource on the topic of Trust:

Trauma erodes our trust in every area of life

Definition of Trust[1]

- assured reliance on the character, ability, strength, or truth of someone or something
- one in which confidence is placed
- dependence on something future or contingent : hope
- a property interest held by one person for the benefit of another
- a charge or duty imposed in faith or confidence or as a condition of some relationship; something committed or entrusted to one to be used or cared for in the interest of another

The words translated "trust" in the Bible literally mean "a bold, confident, sure security or action based on that security." Trust is not

---

[1] Websters Dictionary

exactly the same as faith, which is the gift of God (Ephesians 2:8-9). Rather, trusting is what we do because of the faith we have been given. Trusting is believing in the promises of God in all circumstances, even in those where the evidence seems to be to the contrary. Hebrews 11 talks about faith, which is accepting and believing the truth that God reveals about Himself, supremely in the person of His Son, the Lord Jesus Christ. Nevertheless, the practical consequence of faith in God is trust, which we prove by living out our full acceptance of God's promises day by day. Furthermore, it is by this trust that we are promised peace: "You will keep in peace him whose mind is steadfast, because he trusts in you" (Isaiah 26:3).

The classic verse regarding trust is Proverbs 3:5: "Trust in the LORD with all your heart and lean not on your own understanding." This verse sums up the Bible's teaching on trust. First, it is the Lord in whom we are to trust, not ourselves or our plans, and certainly not the world's wisdom and devices. We trust in the Lord because He and He alone is truly trustworthy. His Word is trustworthy (Psalm 93:5; 111:7; Titus 1:9), His nature is faithful and true (Deuteronomy 7:9; Psalm 25:10; 145:13; 146:6), and His plans for us are perfect and purposeful (Isaiah 46:10; Jeremiah 29:11). Further, because of God's nature, we are to trust Him with all our hearts, committing every aspect of our lives to Him in complete confidence. Finally, we are not to trust in ourselves because our understanding is temporal, finite, and tainted by our sin natures. Trusting in ourselves is like walking confidently across a rotten wooden bridge over a yawning chasm thousands of feet deep. Disaster inevitably follows.

Trust in God is a feature of many of the psalms of David. There are 39 references to trust in the Psalms alone, whether referring to trusting in God and His Word, or to not trusting in riches or the things of this world. It is on the basis of this trust that David finds deliverance from all the evil he encounters. Many of David's psalms describe situations when he was pursued by Saul and his army, as well as his other enemies, and always did the Lord come to his aid. One thing that can be noted about biblical trust is that it always engenders further trust in our God. The man of God never stops trusting in God completely. His faith may be knocked, He may stumble, or He may fall into the foulest of sins, but "though he stumble, he will not fall, for the LORD upholds him with his hand" (Psalm 37:24). The man of God knows that, though trials will beset in this life, his trust will not waiver because that trust is based on faith in the promises of God: the promise of eternal joy with the Lord and the promise of an inheritance that "can never perish, spoil and fade" (1 Peter 1:4).[2]

"O keep me, Lord, and deliver me; let me not

---

[2] gotanswers.org

be ashamed or disappointed, for my trust and my refuge are in You."
Psalm 25:20 AMP

"It is better to trust and take refuge in the Lord than to put confidence in man."
Psalm 118:8 AMP

"For You are my hope; O Lord God, You are my trust from my youth and the source of my confidence."
Psalm 71:5 AMP

"And they who know Your name [who have experience and acquaintance with Your mercy] will lean on and confidently put their trust in You, for You, Lord, have not forsaken those who seek (inquire of and for) You [on the authority of God's Word and the right of their necessity]. [Ps. 42:1.]"
Psalm 9:10 AMP

"And they who know Your name [who have experience and acquaintance with Your mercy] will lean on and confidently put their trust in You, for You, Lord, have not forsaken those who seek (inquire of and for) You [on the authority of God's Word and the right of their necessity]. [Ps. 42:1.]"
Psalm 9:10 AMP

"SING, O barren one, you who did not bear; break forth into singing and cry aloud, you who did not travail with child! For the [spiritual] children of the desolate one will be more than the children of the married wife, says the Lord. [Gal. 4:27.] Enlarge the place of your tent, and let the curtains of your habitations be stretched out; spare not; lengthen your cords and strengthen your stakes, For you will spread abroad to the right hand and to the left; and your offspring will possess the nations and make the desolate cities to be inhabited. Fear not, for you shall not be ashamed; neither be confounded and depressed, for you shall not be put to shame. For you shall forget the shame of your youth, and you shall not [seriously] remember the reproach of your widowhood any more. For your Maker is your Husband–the Lord of hosts is His name–and the Holy One of Israel is your Redeemer; the God of the whole earth He is called. For the Lord has called you like a woman forsaken, grieved in spirit, and heartsore–even a wife [wooed and won] in youth, when she is [later] refused and scorned, says your God. For a brief moment I forsook you, but with great compassion and mercy I will gather you [to Me] again. In a little burst of wrath I hid My face from you for a moment, but with age-enduring love and kindness I will have compassion and mercy on you, says the Lord, your Redeemer. For this is like the days of Noah to Me; as I swore that the waters of Noah should no more go over the earth, so have I sworn that I will not be angry with you or rebuke you. For though the mountains should depart and the hills be shaken or removed, yet My love and kindness shall not depart from you, nor shall My covenant of peace and completeness be removed, says the Lord, Who has compassion on you. O you afflicted [city], storm-tossed and not comforted, behold, I will set your stones in fair colors [in antimony to enhance their brilliance] and lay your foundations with sapphires. And I will make your windows and pinnacles of [sparkling] agates or rubies, and your gates of [shining] carbuncles, and all your walls [of your enclosures] of precious stones. [Rev. 21:19-21.] And all your [spiritual] children shall be disciples [taught by the Lord and obedient to His will], and great shall be the peace and undisturbed composure of your children. [John 6:45.] You shall establish yourself in righteousness (rightness, in conformity with God's will and order): you shall be far from even the thought of oppression or destruction, for you shall not fear, and from terror, for it shall not come near you. Behold, they may gather together and stir up strife, but it is not from Me. Whoever stirs up strife

against you shall fall and surrender to you. Behold, I have created the smith who blows on the fire of coals and who produces a weapon for its purpose; and I have created the devastator to destroy. But no weapon that is formed against you shall prosper, and every tongue that shall rise against you in judgment you shall show to be in the wrong. This [peace, righteousness, security, triumph over opposition] is the heritage of the servants of the Lord [those in whom the ideal Servant of the Lord is reproduced]; this is the righteousness or the vindication which they obtain from Me [this is that which I impart to them as their justification], says the Lord."
Isaiah 54:1-17 AMP

Reestablishing Trust 21 Day Devotional
All rights reserved Tami Rene' Demers 2019

Bible verses from the Passion Translation and the New King James

About the Author

Tami has lived in North Central Washington area most of her life. She is married to Jim, has 3 grown children and 4 grandchildren. She desires to empower people through equipping and training so their God-given destinies can flourish to grow to be a blessing to others through diversity rather than conformity. A passion to see people walking in wholeness and freedom spiritually, in their souls and practically in everyday life. To release hope one heart at a time. Through yielding to the Lord Jesus and the renewing of the mind (Romans 12:1-2) through His Word people begin to see and experience things from a higher perspective which restores hope in their lives bringing transformation.

She mentors, teaches and equips people from a Biblical Pastoral perspective filled with hope and encouragement grounded in relationship with Jesus and empowerment of the Holy Spirit. Having been healed herself from so much adversity she shares insights to bring others into the their own deeper intimate relationship with their Father in Heaven.

Testimonials:

You give hope. You point people to Jesus. You tell the truth. You don't sugar-coat things. You make me feel encouraged, supported, loved, accepted. You have a servant's heart. You freely give what you have received. You have overcome so much, and with those victories you have become very strong and help others understand that they, too, can be an overcomer. You are bold, not afraid to take risks. You give with no expectation of receiving anything in return. "J"

You have a heart like Jesus and a BIG EAR that takes time to listen. You have this ability of really fine tuning your ears to hear what others have to say so you can go direct to the root of the issue to remove and cast out what is not of God in the situation and release the word and promises of God into lives and situations. "A"

Journal Page:

Journal Page:

Journal Page:

Journal Page:

_____

_____

_____

_____

_____

_____

_____

_____

_____

_____

_____

_____

_____

_____

_____

_____

_____

_____

_____

_____

Journal Page:

_____

_____

_____

_____

_____

_____

_____

_____

_____

_____

_____

_____

_____

_____

_____

_____

_____

_____

_____

_____

_____

Journal Page:

Journal Page:

Journal Page:

Journal Page: